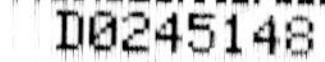

The Three Little SUPERPIGS

Written and Illustrated by
Claire Evans

For my gorgeous Lucy and Amy x

fourth wall
publishing

First published in Great Britain by Fourth Wall Publishing in 2016.

ISBN: 978-1-910851-24-1

A CIP catalogue record for this title is available from the British Library.

Once upon a time, there were three little pigs who captured the Big Bad Wolf when he was trying to eat them! He fell bottom-first, down their chimney into a big pan of boiling water!

"I'll get you one day little pigs!"
shouted the angry Wolf
as he was carted off to prison.

As a thank you for defeating the nasty villain, the pigs were awarded superhero 'Superpig' status by the grateful citizens of Fairyland, and they helped to rebuild the whole town out of bricks to keep everybody safe.

"We love you Superpigs!!"

From that moment on, the Superpigs spent all their days fighting crime and stopping nursery rhyme bad guys...

...but mostly, there was one hard-working, clever pig who did all the work, whilst his brothers just revelled in their new-found fame.

On the other side of town in his dark, dreary cell, the very angry Big Bad Wolf was hungrily plotting his revenge.

CEMENT MIXING
The Art of
Bricklaying for Dummies
How to Build a Wall

A few weeks later, the Superpigs were called to investigate a new crime. Mysteriously, one by one, bricks were starting to disappear all around Fairyland.

The pigs were VERY puzzled...

Then they received some shocking news...

THE BIG BAD WOLF HAD ESCAPED!

The residents of Fairyland were terrified
and once again turned to the Superpigs for help.
"Don't worry!" said the pigs.
"We'll find that Wolf and make him pay!"

They hunted high and low, far and wide,
but The Big Bad Wolf was nowhere to be seen.

Deep Dark
Woods

The pigs searched everywhere for clues!

Some people claimed they'd seen
the Wolf dressed up as an old lady...

...so the pigs rounded up all of the Grandmas in Fairyland.

But the Wolf was a master of disguise and they just couldn't spot him!

As night fell,
the townspeople locked themselves
indoors, too frightened to go out.
Everyone hoped the pigs would
find the Wolf soon.

WANTED
HAVE YOU SEEN

Inside his own home, the first Superpig was relaxing, when a dark shadow suddenly fell upon the room...

"THE BIG BAD WOLF!!"
cried the little pig!

In a panic, he ran all around the house
and out through the front door!
But he was met with a terrible surprise!...

The cunning Wolf had built
a gigantic wall around the pigs' houses
using the stolen bricks from Fairyland!
They were surrounded!

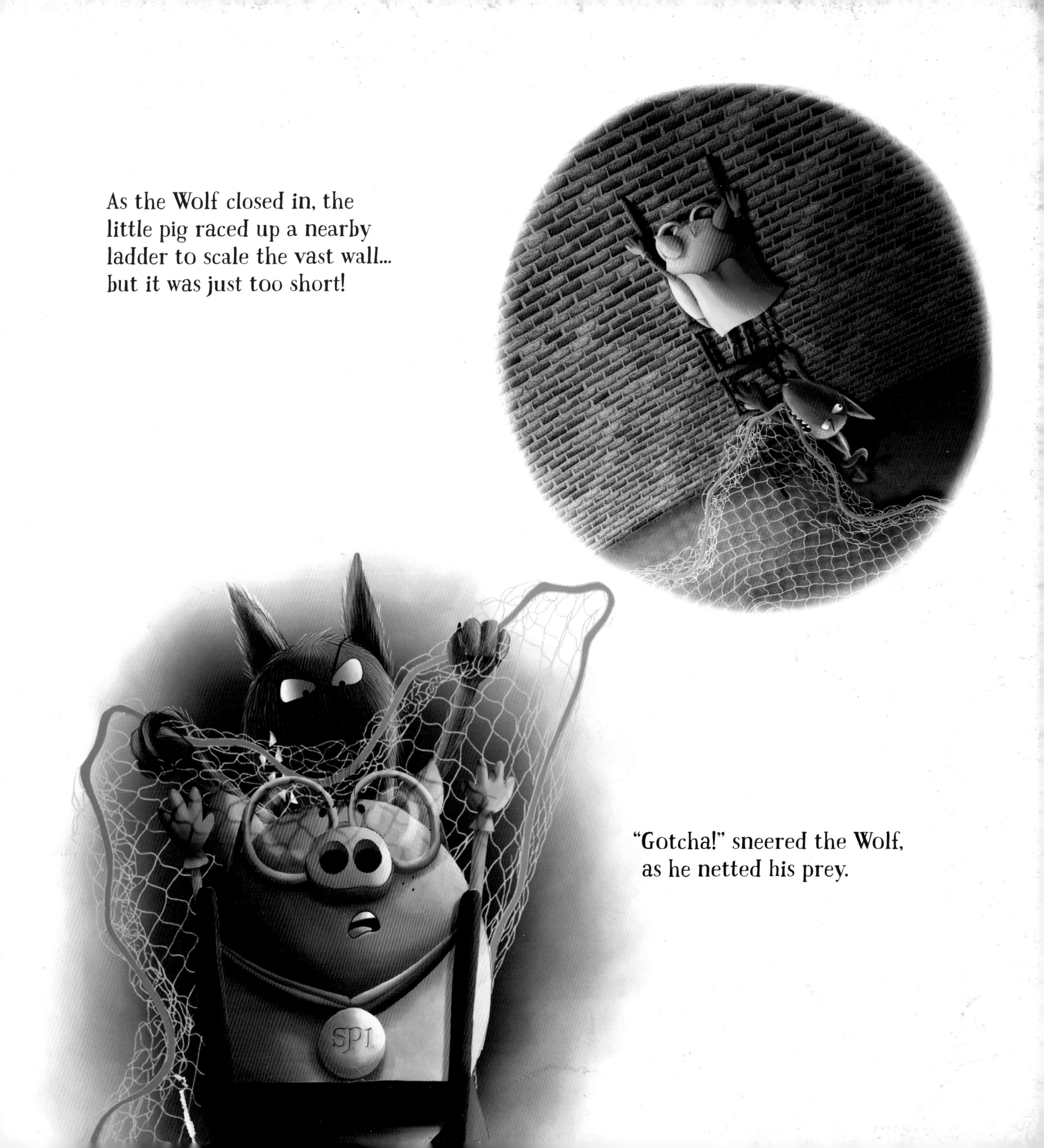

As the Wolf closed in, the little pig raced up a nearby ladder to scale the vast wall... but it was just too short!

"Gotcha!" sneered the Wolf, as he netted his prey.

Unaware of the danger, the second Superpig was at home polishing his medals, when he suddenly spotted something out of the corner of his eye...

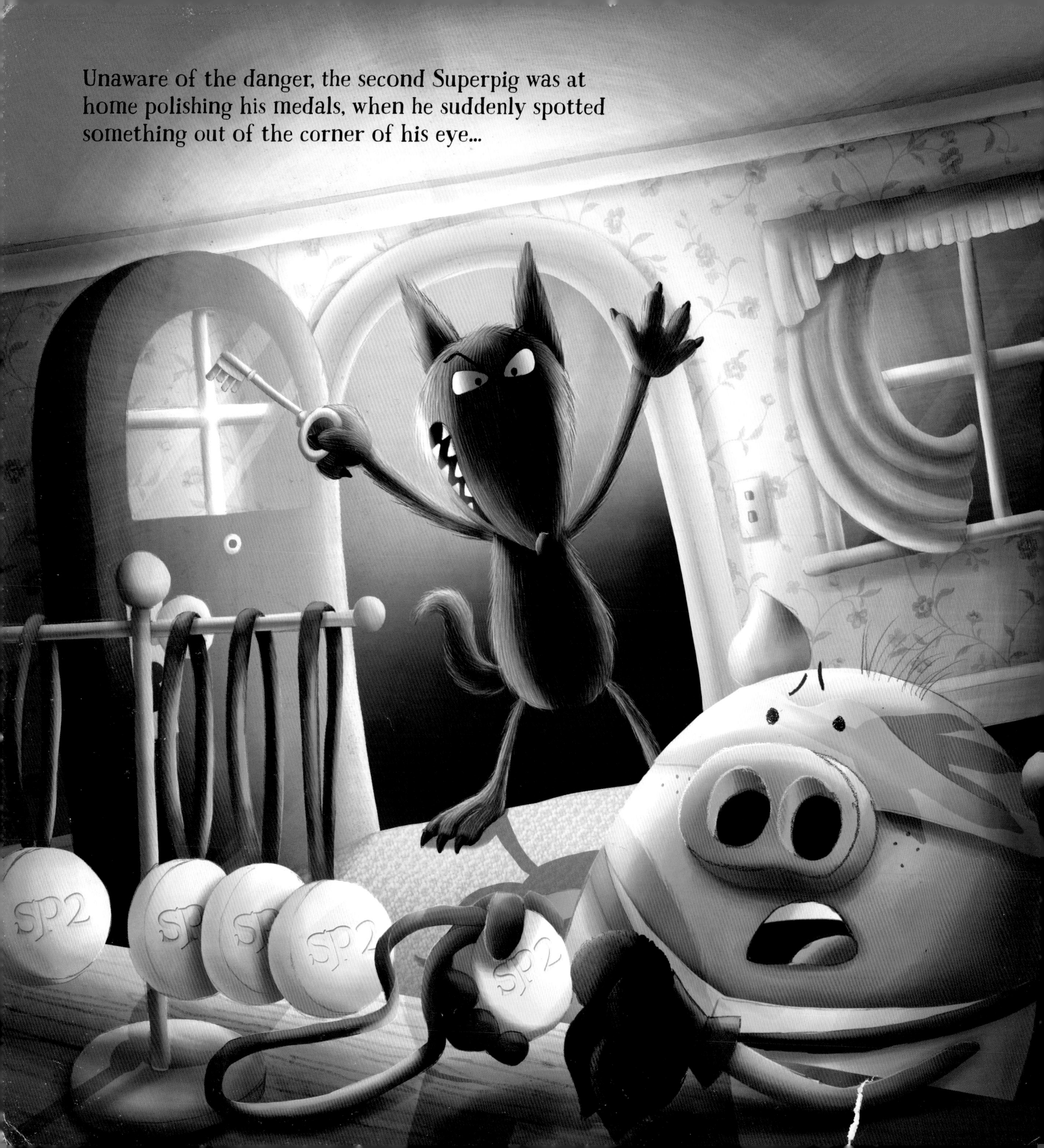

"THE BIG BAD
WOLF!!"

shrieked the little pig.

Terrified, he let out a scream
and ran through his front door...
but he too got a nasty shock when
he saw the enormous, high wall!

Desperate to escape, the little pig jumped on a nearby trampoline, bouncing as high as he could... but it was no use!

"Gotcha!" boasted the Wolf, catching the poor little pig in his trusty net.

"Two down, one to go!"
laughed the Wolf menacingly
as he prepared his delicious meal.

The third Superpig had heard the commotion
and was busy hatching a plan when
the Big Bad Wolf suddenly appeared at his window.

With a plan in mind, he raced straight out of his front door and past the Wolf – as quick as his little legs could carry him.

Working quickly, he freed his captured brothers from their tight pastry blankets, just as the scary Wolf caught up.

"HA HA HA!...There's nowhere to run
and nowhere to hide!
I've built a wall around your houses
and now you're trapped inside!"
laughed the hungry Wolf.

"I DON'T THINK SO!" shouted
The Three Little Superpigs!
And in a flash...

...they blasted off, high into the night sky!

Once more, the clever pig
had used his inventions to save the day
by creating jetpacks for him and his brothers.

The Superpigs had outsmarted the silly Wolf
who was trapped far below
inside his own self-built prison!

SP1
SP3
SP2

"Wow, pigs really can fly!"

SP1
SP3
SP2
The pigs were heroes and
had saved Fairyland again!
"Hurray for The Three Little Superpigs!"